In Trouble

A Brush with Trouble
by Franzeska G Ewart 3

Illustrated by Susan Hellard

Mr Crump
by Tim Bowler 23

Illustrated by Debbie Hinks

The Miracle of the Dishcloths
by Sean Taylor 43

Illustrated by Jennifer Ward

Rigby, Halley Court, Jordan Hill, Oxford, OX2 8EJ
a division of Reed Educational and Professional Publishing Ltd
www.rigbyed.co.uk

Rigby is a registered trademark of Reed Educational and Professional
Publishing Ltd

In Trouble first published 2002

Series editor: Wendy Wren

06 05 04 03 02
10 9 8 7 6 5 4 3 2 1

In Trouble   ISBN 0433 07803 0
Group Reading Pack with Teaching Notes   ISBN 0433 07809 X

Illustrated by Susan Hellard, Debbie Hinks, Jennifer Ward
Cover illustration © Philip Hurst 2002
Repro by Digital Imaging, Glasgow
Printed in Great Britain by Ashford Colour Press, Gosport, Hants.

A Brush with Trouble

by Franzeska G Ewart

Mike and Angelo were twins. They lived with their mum in a neat and tidy street called Oak Grove, surrounded by neat and tidy neighbours. The neighbours took great pride in their gardens, which were as neat and as tidy as you could possibly imagine.

Mike and Angelo's garden, however, was anything but neat and tidy. That was because their mum was an artist and the garden was where she did her paintings.

Mum's paintings were not the sort you would look at and say, "What a very realistic horse!" or "What a beautiful lake!" They were modern paintings and that meant, when you looked at them, you often didn't know what to say.

It was fun watching Mum painting. She would hang up a sheet on the fence and cover her palette with big blobs of paint. Then she would load three paintbrushes with glistening globs of colour, stick one of the paintbrushes behind her ear and hold the other two in front of her like sticky swords.

The paintbrushes would be so full of quivering paint that it would drip over Mum's face, her shirt, Constable the dog and, of course, the garden. With a great cry of, *"PICASSOOOO!"* she would charge at the sheet, waving the paintbrushes around wildly. Usually, some paint would manage to land on the sheet, and that was the start of a modern painting. Mike and Angelo loved to watch her, occasionally cheering her on.

Mum also did sculptures, but her sculptures weren't the sort of sculptures you would look at and say, "Just look at the muscles on that man!" or "Wouldn't you swear that lion could roar?" Mum's sculptures might be a pile of bricks with a pair of red socks on top, under an inverted goldfish bowl, called 'Climb Every Mountain'; or a bath full of treacle, with a flotilla of yellow plastic ducks on its surface, called 'The Black Sea'.

So the garden, as well as being covered in paint, was full of strange objects with labels by them to tell you what to think they were.

Mike and Angelo loved to watch Mum at work. They never knew what was going to happen next, and there was always the chance of getting involved. One time she decided to smear them with syrup, roll them in popcorn, and call them 'Sweet Dreams Are Made of These'.

Although Mike and Angelo were extremely keen on modern art, there were times when they did wish they had a neat and tidy mother. They also wished they had a neat and tidy garden they could actually grow things in and so, one summer's day, they came up with an idea.

"If we can't have a nice garden ourselves ... " announced Mike,

" ... we will dedicate our lives to the improvement of other people's gardens," declared Angelo.

"We will combine our artistic inspiration with our horticultural knowledge ... " continued Mike,

" ... to create unique works of art within the gardens of Oak Grove!" finished Angelo.

And they set off to do just that.

They found a wheelbarrow, painted it bright blue, and nailed on a notice that said, 'Mike and Angelo, GARDEN ARTISTS'.

In the wheelbarrow they put all the things a Garden Artist would need: hedge-clippers, a broom, trowels, paint, paintbrushes, and so on.

Mum, meanwhile, was engrossed in the sculpture she was entering for the annual Turnbull Prize. So she didn't notice as, each holding a handle, the twins set off squeakily down Oak Grove.

The first house Mike and Angelo stopped outside was *Dunroamin,* the home of Colonel Pickering. Colonel Pickering was ferociously proud of his privet hedge, and had cut it into wonderful shapes – peacocks, spirals, and neat little trees like French poodles.

Mike and Angelo looked at the hedge thoughtfully.

"Look, Angelo," Mike said, "there's a great big bit at the end which ... "

" ... isn't cut into a shape," added Angelo.

"It's so boring," Mike went on. "I think we ought to ... "

" ... jazz it up," finished Angelo.

"It's a job for Mike and Angelo, Garden Artists!" they chorused, as they dived into their wheelbarrow and took out the hedge-clippers. Mike began to cut.

"How about a dragon with a ... "

" ... long neck," said Angelo. After a few minutes they stood back to admire Mike's work. It didn't look much like a dragon at all. It looked more like ...

" ... a hamster," said Angelo, reaching for the hedge-clippers.

Suddenly the door burst open and Colonel Pickering came out, shaking his fist at the twins. "What the devil do you think you're doing to my hedge?" he shouted.

Mike and Angelo couldn't understand why Colonel Pickering seemed so angry. Perhaps, they thought, it was because the hedge looked more like a hamster than a dragon.

"We haven't finished ... " said Angelo.

" ... the dragon," added Mike, pulling the hedge-clippers away from Angelo.

"It *will* look like a dragon ... " Angelo went on,

" ... when we've made its neck longer," Mike said, giving a large *clip!* to show what he meant.

Colonel Pickering's face turned from red to puce to purple and his hair bristled like Mum's biggest paintbrush when it was covered in Titanium White.

"I do not want a dragon, or anything else!" he exploded. "All I want is for you to pick up every single hedge-clipping and GO!"

Mike and Angelo looked at one another, aghast. "But Colonel Pickering— " they said, "we thought you'd like it."

They took a large broom out of the blue wheelbarrow and swept up the hedge-clippings in stunned silence. When the wheelbarrow was full and they were squeaking their way down Oak Grove, they looked back at Colonel Pickering's hedge. If you half-closed your eyes, you could almost see a dragon.

"There's no pleasing some people," sighed Angelo.

"That's what Mum says," agreed Mike.

After a while, Angelo stopped. They were outside the garden of *Thistle Dhu*, where Miss McPeak lived. Miss McPeak was very fond of garden gnomes, and was famed throughout Oak Grove for her collection.

Sometimes, if they were careful to wipe their feet first, she let Mike and Angelo walk around and look at them.

There were gnomes with fishing rods and gnomes with bunches of flowers. There were gnomes sitting, gnomes standing and gnomes lying down. Some gnomes played musical instruments and some watered their own little gardens. There were tiny gnomes, middle-sized gnomes and big gnomes.

"There's no place like gnome," observed Mike.

"Haven't you got a gnome to go to?" smiled Angelo.

Angelo pointed to a group of gnomes by the side of the fishpond. "Just look at them, Mike," he said. "They're practically ... "

" ... bare," added Mike.

"That's right," Angelo went on. "What they need is a good ... "

" ... lick of paint!" finished Mike.

"It's another job for Mike and Angelo, Garden Artists!" they chorused.

They unloaded tubes of paint and paintbrushes and wiped their feet thoroughly on the edge of the lawn. Angelo fetched the gnomes that were most in need of a makeover.

Miss McPeak's gnomes all had green clothes so Mike and Angelo decided it would be refreshing to have a bit of a change. They gave the gnomes Magenta jackets and Prussian Blue trousers, and they painted their faces a nice Burnt Sienna.

"Better than pink," said Mike.

"Healthier-looking," agreed Angelo.

They had
almost finished,
and the gnomes
were lined up
smartly waiting to
dry, when a window
opened and a face appeared.
At first, Mike and Angelo didn't recognise
who it was. The normally sedate Miss McPeak
had changed into a howling banshee. Every
hairpin had dislodged itself from her hair,
which flew wildly around like a grey mist.

"If Ah wasnae seein' this wi' ma ane e'en,"
she wailed, "Ah widnae believe it! Jist whit dae
ye think ye're daein' tae ma gnomes?"

Mike looked at Angelo, and Angelo looked
at Mike. Birds stopped singing, and a deathly
hush descended. At last Angelo said, very
quietly, "Giving them an artistic makeover,
Miss McPeak."

For a moment it looked as though Miss McPeak would tear her hair out by the roots. She slammed the window shut and appeared a second later at the door. The twins watched in horrified amazement as she picked up the still-sticky gnomes and hurled them one by one into the blue wheelbarrow.

"*Artistic makeover!*" she shouted. "Ah'll gie ye *artistic makeover!*" she roared, tossing the gnomes with surprising accuracy onto their bed of privet cuttings.

When the last gnome had landed, she glared at Mike and Angelo and hissed dangerously, "Try ony mair 'artistic makeovers' in ma gairden, and Ah'm warnin' ye – Ah'll hae yer guts for gairters!"

As Mike and Angelo squeaked sadly up their front path, Mike said, "You know what Mum says, Angelo?"

"What does Mum say, Mike?" Angelo asked miserably.

"She says artists are often misunderstood," Mike said.

"Mum's right," said Angelo, as, dejectedly, they went to wash their hands for lunch.

"Spag bol," said Mum brightly, putting two steaming hot bowls in front of them. As they ate, Mum pointed over to a large dome of chicken wire with rubber gloves stuck in it. The rubber gloves were all different colours and beautifully bright. When Mum turned on a fan below the dome, they filled with air and rose up and down in quite a lifelike way.

"I call it 'A Farewell to Arms'," she said. "What do you think?"

Mike and Angelo smiled through their spag bol and said they thought it was just great.

"I'm entering it for the Turnbull Prize at the Town Hall this afternoon," said Mum. "Think it'll win £50,000?"

Mike and Angelo nodded. "Bound to," they said together.

Just then, the phone rang. Mum picked it up. *"No!"* she said, in a horrified voice, and *"Really!"* and *"Surely not?"* and finally, with a terrible look at Mike and Angelo, "I'LL HAVE A WORD WITH THEM!"

She banged the phone down and glared at the twins. "You have been vandals!" she growled at them. "I am ashamed of you! How could you destroy things that are precious to people?"

"We didn't think we were being vandals, Mum," they said, lips quivering. "We thought we were being Garden Artists."

"We just wanted to combine our ... artistic inspiration with our ... horticultural knowledge," whispered Mike, sobbing in between each word,

" ... to create unique works of art within the gardens of Oak Grove!" squeaked Angelo, dissolving into tears.

"Unique works of art, my hat," Mum muttered furiously. "I want you to go round to Colonel Pickering and Miss McPeak and say you're Very Sorry Indeed. And take Constable. I want rid of the lot of you."

Mike and Angelo slipped shamefacedly out of their seats. They clipped Constable's lead to his collar and set off, taking the blue wheelbarrow with its evidence of their dreadful crimes.

"Perhaps if we did some weeding? Wouldn't that be like offering an olive branch?" said Mike, as they trailed up Oak Grove.

"It might," agreed Angelo, doubtfully. "Though perhaps we shouldn't mention branches."

On the way to *Dunroamin*, Mike grabbed Angelo's sleeve. "Wait!" he hissed. "I have an idea."

"What?" asked Angelo.

"It's just an idea," he said mysteriously. "Maybe," he went on, even more mysteriously, "there's a way we can make it up to Colonel Pickering and Miss McPeak ... "

"How?" asked Angelo.

"You'll see ... " Mike went on, picking up the blue wheelbarrow and squeaking off in the direction of the Town Hall. "Maybe we have more artistic inspiration than we thought we had."

There were crowds of people thronging about inside, and Mum was at a plinth setting up her 'Farewell to Arms' sculpture. Mike crept past her with the wheelbarrow. A puzzled Angelo and a slightly dazed Constable followed.

TOWN HALL

Mike and Angelo GARDEN ARTISTS

Once he was past Mum, Mike steered the wheelbarrow in and out of the throngs of people so that Miss McPeak's gnomes bounced up and down madly. They were so covered in hedge-clippings now that you could only just see their Magenta jackets, and their Prussian Blue trousers, and their Burnt Sienna faces.

At last, Mike stopped at a desk behind which sat a very smart woman. When she saw Mike and Angelo and Constable and the blue wheelbarrow filled with privet-leaf-covered garden gnomes, she leaped up.

"Oh my!" she said, coming out from behind the desk. "Now this *is* special!"

She called over to a man in a black suit. "Nigel! Just look at this!" And they both examined the blue wheelbarrow from every angle.

"It's so – so *vibrant!*" said Nigel at last.

"So full of life— " said the woman.

"And yet so strangely ... *peaceful*," added Nigel.

"Oh, do look at those wonderful little men, Nigel! These must be the 'Garden Artists', at one with Nature, immersed in their art— "

"And don't you just adore the dog?" Nigel added, pointing at Constable, who was sitting bolt upright beside the wheelbarrow. "So *patient,* so *watchful!*"

"Do you know what this sculpture shows us, Nigel?" said the woman, sighing deeply. "It shows us the artist's eternal struggle to add beauty to the leaf-litter of life! It shows us how the artist, weak and tiny in himself, transforms this drab world with his wonderful colours! In short," she finished with tears in her eyes, "this sculpture shows us the very meaning of Art itself!"

The hall had become very quiet. A man with a gold chain round his neck began to speak. "Ladies and gentlemen," he announced, "I now have great pleasure in awarding the Turnbull Prize to Mike and Angelo for their truly ground-breaking sculpture, 'Garden Artists'."

There was a great cheer.

"Speech!" someone called.

"We would like to say … " began Mike.

" … how honoured we are to receive this prize," Angelo went on.

"And we will use some of it to buy Colonel Pickering's new hedge … " said Mike.

" … and to buy Miss McPeak some *de luxe* garden gnomes … " Angelo added.

" … and our mother a state-of-the-art studio!" beamed Mike.

"Furthermore," Angelo went on, "we would like our sculpture to stand in the Square and remind everyone of the importance of Art … "

" … though that won't include Constable," Mike pointed out, as everyone clapped.

And right at the back, streaked with paint, their mum clapped loudest of all.

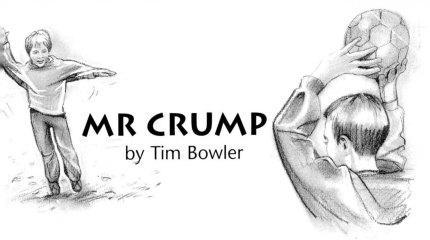

MR CRUMP
by Tim Bowler

Jed looked over at me with his baby-face grin.

"Denny! On me nut!"

I threw him the football and he headed it against the wall of the pub. Across the village square I saw old Mrs Wendell watching disapprovingly. Jed didn't notice her. He was too busy mucking around. You wouldn't have thought he was ten. He acted more like his five-year-old brother, who was as daft as a brush, but I suppose I wasn't much better. Whenever Dad ticked me off for something – which was most days – he usually ended up giving the same old lecture. "You're ten now, Denny. Double figures. It's time to grow up."

But growing up didn't seem like a bundle of fun to me.

"Let's go and wind up Crump," I said.

"Good idea," Jed grinned.

Winding up Crump was always a good laugh. He was a miserable old man who snapped at everyone who came near his house, especially scruffy urchins like Jed and me. But that didn't stop us going. In fact, it was half the fun. There was a patch of grass by his house that we liked to use for a kick-about, but what was really great was that it always brought the old man out fuming.

We cut down the lane that led to his house. It was tucked away at the bottom all by itself and Crump never seemed to leave it, except to go to the post office for his pension and to buy food, and to rub everybody up the wrong way. Jed started bouncing the ball as we drew near.

"Just to let him know we're coming," he said with a wink.

I saw the old man sitting by the window, staring out. He caught sight of us and stood up at once.

"Here we go," I said. "Get ready for fireworks!"

We ran round to the grass, but before Jed could even kick the ball, I heard the front door open and the old man's peppery voice.

"Clear off!"

"This isn't your land!" shouted Jed.

The old man was stumbling towards the garden fence, his face twisted with rage. "You little snipes!" he screamed. "You don't give a damn about anything!"

"This isn't your land," said Jed again. "We can play football here if we want to. Denny!" He kicked the ball up into the air.

But to my horror, he sliced it off the outside of his foot and instead of coming in my direction, the ball flew straight into Crump's front garden. The old man gave a snarl of triumph, snatched up the ball, and took it back into the house.

"Give us our ball back!" I shouted, but he closed the door behind him without a word. I turned furiously to Jed. "You idiot!"

"Sorry, Denny. I didn't mean to. What are we going to do now?"

"I don't know."

"He'll have to give it back. It's yours," Jed frowned. "You could get your dad to come over."

"I can't say anything about this at home. Dad's always giving me stick for winding up Crump. Look, I'd better get back. I need to think what to do."

But I already knew what that was, and by the next morning I'd plucked up the courage for it. I caught Jed outside his house as he was setting off for the school bus.

"I'm mitching today," I said.

"What?"

"Going to get my ball back from Crump."

"And how are you going to do that?" said Jed. "Ask him? 'Oh, Mr Crump, it's so nice to see you. Can I have my ball back, please?'"

"I'm going to break in to his house."

Jed gasped. "Is this a joke?"

"It's pension day." I said. "He always goes to the post office. I'll hide behind the fence and wait till he goes out."

"And how are you going to break in?"

"Don't know yet," I said, trying to sound braver than I felt. "Smash a window maybe. I'll think of something."

"But if you take the ball, he'll know it was you," said Jed.

"I'm only taking what's mine. I'm not going to touch anything else."

"And what are you going to tell your parents when they find out you've bunked off school?" asked Jed.

"I haven't thought that far ahead."

"You're nuts, Denny." Jed gave a sigh. "OK, let's go."

"What?"

"I'm coming with you. Wouldn't miss it for the world."

We waited until the school bus had gone, then ran down to Crump's house. The curtains were still drawn.

"Good," I said. "He's still asleep. Let's get into position."

We ran round the side of the front garden, slid to the ground with our backs to the fence, and waited. An hour passed, then another, and still the curtains remained drawn.

"Taking his time getting up," said Jed.

I heard an engine in the lane and peeped through a gap in the fence.

"Postman."

The van pulled up outside the house and the postman climbed out.

"He's got a parcel," I said, still squinting through the gap. "That'll bring the old boy to the door."

But there was no answer from the house. The postman rang several times. Finally, he put a card through the door, took the parcel back to the van, and drove off.

I looked round at Jed. "Crump's been out all the time."

"Maybe he's still asleep and didn't hear the bell."

"It's half-ten, Jed. Even you don't sleep that long. Come on."

We ran round the side of the house and pressed ourselves against the wall. "See if there's a window open at the back," I said. "I'll keep watch here."

Jed ran off but soon returned. "No problem. The back door's unlocked."

I felt a sudden flutter of fear. I didn't know why. After all, this was turning out to be so easy – yet something felt wrong. Jed looked edgy, too, though he didn't say anything. I clenched my fists and led the way round the back and into the house.

It was a smelly place, and there was dirt everywhere. The kitchen was so filthy that it turned my stomach, but the weirdest thing was that there didn't seem to be any food around, apart from some mouldy crusts of bread on the table, and a half-finished pack of biscuits. The draining board was covered in dust, and the cooker draped with cobwebs. There was no sign of the football.

We crept through to the sitting room. All we found there was a battered old television and some tatty furniture. No pictures, ornaments, books – only more dust, more cobwebs, and no football. Jed turned to me.

"It must be upstairs."

He'd spoken firmly enough, but his eyes betrayed his fear and I knew he'd stop right there. Jed's confidence never went further than his mouth.

"OK," I said. "I'll check it out. Wait in the hall."

Slowly, warily, I made my way up the stairs. With every step I took, the feeling of certainty grew that this house – for all its ghostly stillness – was not empty at all. I reached the top and stopped, breathing hard.

Down below I saw Jed looking up, his face etched with tension. I turned back to the landing.

There were only two doors. I braced myself and pushed open the first. It was a pokey little bathroom with a cracked basin and a loo with a broken seat. A threadbare towel hung from the rail, and a toothbrush and a bar of soap lay on a shelf. I walked towards the second door.

I was trembling now. I couldn't stop myself. I knew the football had to be in this room, but if Crump was in the house, he'd be here too. I braced myself again, pushed open the door and peered in. There was the ball on the floor – and to my relief, no sign of Crump.

"Jed!" I shouted. "I've found it! And Crump's not here!"

Jed bounded up and joined me. "Grab it and let's go."

I bent down to pick up the ball, then stiffened.

"What's up?" said Jed.

I nodded towards the far side of the room.

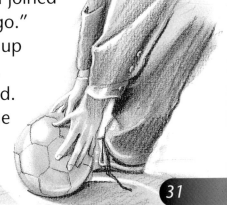

There, lying on the floor, half-hidden by the bed, was the figure of Mr Crump, his eyes closed, his mouth gaping, his cheeks as pale as death.

Jed grabbed me by the arm.

"Let's get out of here."

"We can't," I said. "We've got to do something."

"He might just be sleeping."

"He's not. You can see that. He's had a heart attack or a stroke or something."

I forced myself to walk over to the body and kneel down. The old man was lying on his back, his chest moving in a horrible jerky way.

"Jed, we've got to ring for an ambulance."

"But we'll get involved. We're not supposed to be here."

"He could die!" I glared at him. "Go and find the phone and ring for an ambulance."

With obvious reluctance, Jed ran off down the stairs. He soon called up again. "There's no phone!"

"Run back to your house and ring from there."

"But Mum'll ask me why I'm not in school."

"Then use the payphone outside the pub!" I shouted.

"I haven't got any money."

"You don't need any! You just dial 999!"

"But— "

"Jed, just do it, can't you?"

I heard the back door slam shut and the sound of Jed haring up the lane.

I looked back at Crump, unsure what to do.
"Mr Crump! Wake up!"

He didn't stir.

"Mr Crump!" But it was no good. He seemed to be slipping away. I thought of Mum at home. A five-minute sprint and I could hand this whole mess over to her.

Suddenly the old man coughed.

"Mr Crump!" I shook him. "You've got to wake up!" He moaned, then suddenly he spluttered, and saliva appeared at the corner of his mouth. His eyes struggled open. They were watery and blurred and I saw a trace of annoyance in them. Whether it was from being shaken, or just the sight of me, I couldn't tell. I didn't suppose he was pleased to see me. With an effort, I heaved him upright until he was slumped against the wall.

"I'll get you some water," I said.

I ran down to the kitchen, cleaned and filled a cup, and hurried back.

"Drink this." I held the cup to his mouth but he showed no interest in it. He just stared glassily at the wall. I put the cup to his lips and tipped it slightly.

Most of the water trickled over his chin, but

some seemed to be going down the right way. Suddenly he pushed the cup away.

I waited a moment, then pulled my handkerchief out and wiped his mouth and chest, where some of the water had spilled. He leaned back and I saw his eyes trying to close again.

"Don't sleep," I said. "Please. You might not wake up again."

I don't know if he heard me but his eyes stayed open, somehow, and he went on staring at the wall.

"Mr Crump?"

No response.

"Mr Crump?" I hesitated. "I'm … sorry about the football. And all the times I've wound you up and stuff."

Again, no answer.

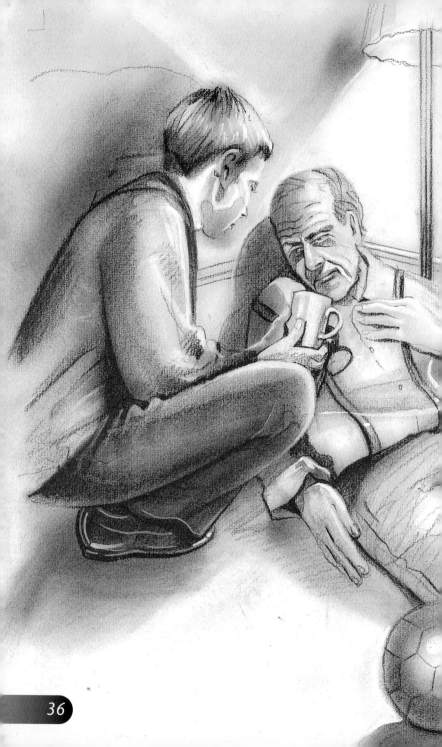

I studied the old man's face. It didn't look angry. It just looked … miserable. Yes, that was it. Miserable. And suddenly I realised I'd never really understood that word before. We'd always called Crump a miserable old whatsit because that's what he was: mean, grumpy – miserable. But the word meant something else, too, something I'd never really thought about until then: it meant wretched, unhappy, broken-hearted. He was all those things as well. I could see it. I bit my lip.

"Mr Crump, I'm sorry I've been horrible to you. It's just that … I'm a bit scared of you and it makes me try and act big. And Jed's scared of you as well. He'll never admit it, but he is. And I think maybe lots of people in the village are scared of you and that's why they're not very nice to you."

There was a long silence, then his eyes blinked and he gave a cough, and then he was still again. I looked at the tired old face.

"Don't die, Mr Crump," I said.

I heard the door bang downstairs, then Jed called up.

"The ambulance is on its way! I'll wait in the lane!"

Ten minutes later, the paramedics rushed in, asked me the briefest of questions, checked Crump over, and whisked him off to hospital.

I didn't go with them. I ran home and poured out the story to Mum. By the end of it I was crying. Mum pulled me close.

"How many times have Dad and I told you not to wind up Mr Crump?"

"I'm sorry. I'm really sorry." And I was, too. I felt as though guilt and pain were going to swallow me up forever, and I was terrified the old man was going to die. I clung to Mum, sobbing. She held me for a while in silence. Then she spoke again, and this time her voice was softer.

"You did wrong, Denny."

"I know."

"But when you found Mr Crump, you did right. OK? And I'm proud of you for that."

I found I couldn't answer. I just went on sobbing.

Mum waited till I'd calmed down, then she spoke again. "So, where's the football?"

I looked up with a start. "I left it behind. Forgot all about it."

"I'll go back and get it if you want," she said. "If the house is still unlocked."

"Don't. It doesn't matter." I wiped my eyes. "Mum, is Mr Crump going to die?"

"Depends on how bad a state he's in. What did he look like?"

I thought of the glazed eyes, the gaping mouth, the laboured breathing. But only one word came to my mind. The same word as before.

"Miserable," I said. "Yeah. Miserable."

"Well, I suppose you'd be miserable if you'd been through what he's been through," said Mum.

"What do you mean?"

"He was tortured in a prisoner-of-war camp during the Second World War. You don't just get over something like that."

"You never told me."

"It's not something many people know about," said Mum. "I only heard about it the other day from Mrs Wendell. She's been really worried about him. She said he'd more or less stopped eating. Like he'd lost the will to live. No wonder his body gave up on him."

I felt the tears start again. Mum stroked my head. "Easy now."

"But— "

"Sssh." She kissed me. "Enough tears."

"Dad'll kill me."

"No, he won't. It'll be all right."

I held her tight. "How come Mrs Wendell knows so much?"

"She's Mr Crump's sister-in-law. She's known him for over sixty years. She said he went away to the war, and came back a different man. And that's the man we thought we knew."

In the afternoon, the police turned up to speak to me. They said Crump had suffered a stroke but was going to survive. He was going to be kept in hospital for a while. They said he'd eaten so little for so long, it was a wonder he hadn't collapsed ages ago.

I didn't get into trouble. In fact, they praised me – told me I'd done well, said he'd probably have died if I hadn't found him when I did.

It didn't make me feel pleased with myself.

It just made me feel strange. I wondered what the old man would be like next time we met, whether he'd shout and swear at me and be horrible again, or whether we'd talk. For some reason I wanted us to talk.

A few days later Mum called me to her. She was standing by the front door, holding my football.

"Where did you get that?" I asked.

"It was left outside the door. With this."

She held out a piece of paper with the word *Denny* scrawled at the top and a short message underneath.

Thank you.
Arthur Crump.

"He's back, then," I said, but Mum shook her head.

"He's been taken to a nursing home. Mrs Wendell just rang and told me."

"So I can't see him?"

"Do you want to?"

I thought for a moment, then nodded. "Yeah."

"He probably won't be any different," she said.

"I know."

"Still grumpy and snappy. And miserable."

"I know."

She watched me for a moment and it seemed to me that her eyes were smiling, though her lips were tight together. Then she reached out and ruffled my hair.

"OK," she said.

THE MIRACLE OF THE DISHCLOTHS

by Sean Taylor

São Paulo, Brazil

The traffic-lights went red and I set off between the lines of cars as they pulled up along the avenue. The sun was hot on my neck, and the back of my T-shirt was soaked in sweat.

There were three of us trying to sell things to the motorists. Up ahead, an old man in a dusty baseball cap went shuffling along, waving a bunch of mobile-phone rechargers. He was one of the regulars. Mr Oswaldo. Behind me was a boy I'd not seen before. He was tall and thin, a bit like me, and was selling chewing gum from a box balanced in one hand.

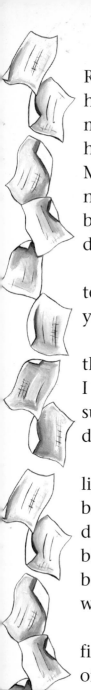

I was selling dishcloths. Three for two Reais. My mum had made about a hundred of the things. Then she had made me go out and sell them. I should have been with my friends at school but Mum wouldn't let me go. She said we needed the money. She said I could go back to school when I'd sold all the dishcloths.

"They're lovely white cloths," she kept telling me. "Clean as a cat's tongue. If you try hard enough, you'll sell the lot."

Well, I'd been walking up and down the traffic every day for three weeks and I still had half of them left. Not surprising perhaps? I mean, who needs a dishcloth when they're driving a car?

I kept trying though. As soon as those lights went red, I went striding up to a big green Renault. There was a woman driving it, with a puffy hairdo like a big bird's nest. A good sign. If anyone bought the dishcloths, it was the women with the puffy hairdos.

But she wasn't looking. She was fiddling around, getting something out of her handbag. Nail-varnish probably.

Or powder for her nose. You know the sort of thing these women spend the whole day doing.

"Madam!" I said. "Three dishcloths for two Reais!"

She looked round hurriedly and smiled at me as if I was a baby in a pram going "gah-gah-gah".

"Not today, my love," she cooed softly at me.

So I walked on. The next car was low and silvery. At the wheel was some kind of businessman, all dressed up in a suit and tie. Well, you could bet your right arm he wasn't sitting there day-dreaming about a new set of dishcloths. But I smiled and I walked towards his car.

The businessman took one look at my smile and clicked all the locks on his car.

I held up a dishcloth.

"Look. As clean as a cat's … "

But I never got any further because there was this loud shout coming from behind me.

I swivelled round and saw Mrs Birdsnest leaning out of her car window and shouting. In the blink of an eye, the boy selling the chewing gum was barging past me, clutching her purse, and running down the line of cars.

"Help!" shrieked Mrs Birdsnest, but the skinny boy had already dodged between the cars and was half-way across the other side of the avenue. I decided to get out of the road myself. Once trouble starts in São Paulo, it's best to make yourself scarce. So I legged it round the silvery car towards the pavement.

Big mistake. A fat man with narrow little piggy eyes stepped out of his car and pointed a finger like a pork sausage at ME.

"Who was it? Him?" he shouted.

"Yes," said Mrs Birdsnest, poking her nose through her car window, "the skinny one who looks like a turkey!"

"It wasn't me!" I protested.

But Piggy Eyes was already stomping towards me with his arms stretched out, looking as if someone had puffed him up with a bicycle pump.

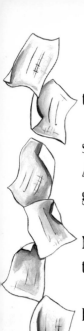

I looked at the businessman.

"You saw!" I shouted. "It was nothing to do with me!"

But my friend in the silvery car just sat there with his lips pushed together. And, by that time, Piggy Eyes had grabbed me by the neck of my T-shirt.

"Oh thank you! Thank you!" shrieked Mrs Birdsnest, craning her head out through the window.

"Where's the purse?" thundered Piggy Eyes.

"It wasn't *me*!"

"Why were you trying to run off, then?" asked Piggy.

With that, he snatched my holdall and tipped the dishcloths out onto the road. No sign of the purse – surprise, surprise!

"You sure it was this one?" he called back to Mrs Birdsnest.

"Yes," came her voice.

"Well he hasn't got a purse!" growled Piggy Eyes.

"He must have!" came Mrs Birdsnest's voice.

"I haven't!" I blurted out. "Let go of me, you great big zombie!"

I could see from the look on Piggy Eyes'
face that he didn't know who to believe.
Anyway, at that moment, the traffic-lights
went green. Engines revved. Horns started
honking. And what did Piggy do? He swung
the empty holdall at me with all his strength.
It whacked into the side of my head. I had
one ear ringing in pain, and the other
deafened by the BEEP-BEEP-BEEP coming
from the silvery car.

"Take your lousy rags! Nobody wants
them! Leave us motorists in peace!" bellowed
Piggy, walking back to his car.

"Why don't you just go home and leave
me alone!" I shouted.

I held up a hand for the cars to wait so that I could pick up the cloths, but it was no use. They were going to run straight at me, so I jumped on the pavement and had to watch as twenty or thirty cars and one 18-wheeler truck ran over the top of my 'lovely white dishcloths'.

Mr Oswaldo came past with a sly grin on his face.

"Silly fool!" he said.

"Who? That man?"

"No," he said "You. I'll eat my hat if you can sell any of those cloths now!"

He was right. When the lights changed I scrabbled between the cars, snatching up all the cloths I could, but they were covered in grit and grime. I felt miserable. My mum was going to wring my neck if I turned up back home with nothing but a bag of dirty dishcloths.

Then something shiny caught my eye on the tarmac. I reached down. It was a ring. Only a tinny thing. Not gold or silver or anything. But I slipped it into my pocket and, as I did, a voice called out, "What happened here?"

A short woman with chubby legs had stopped on the pavement.

"Come on," she said, bending down, "I'll give you a hand."

"Thanks," I nodded and, as she helped, I told her the whole story.

She couldn't stop laughing – especially when I got to the part about the woman saying I looked like a turkey.

"Yeah. Very funny," I said. "And what am I meant to do now? Nobody buys these things even when they're clean!"

"All they need is a good wash," shrugged the woman.

"And how am I going to do that?"

"Let's think ... " she said. "Look, I'm a cleaner up in those apartments over the road. I'm meant to be on my way home. The woman I work for has gone out for the afternoon, so we could nip over and put the cloths in her washing machine."

I think I blurted out, "I love you!" or something. Whatever it was, it made her burst out laughing – a lovely, mischievous sort of laugh, as though she really liked the idea of doing something that she wasn't supposed to.

Moments later, the two of us were crossing the road into the shadows of the great tall apartment blocks lining the avenue. The woman said her name was Sonia. I told her everyone called me Pipoca because of the way I jump about like popcorn when I play in the school football team.

"I bet you don't even go to school!" she said.

"When I can, I do," I protested. "But my dad died last year, and Mum has hardly had any money since then, so sometimes I have to go out and work."

"Watch out, or you'll end up selling things at the traffic-lights for the rest of your life!" Sonia said as we walked up to a big metal gate outside one of the blocks of flats.

There was a security-guard sitting in a little room on the other side of the gate. He looked closely at Sonia, then pressed a button which made the gate swing open.

It was so cool and quiet in the building, it reminded me of a church. The ceiling was about ten times my height and the floor was so shiny I hardly dared to tread on it in my manky old flip-flops. Sonia pressed a button and a lift door swished open. We went right up to the top floor. Sonia said the apartment was so big that it took up a whole floor on its own.

"It must have about four bedrooms!" I said.

Sonia raised her eyebrows. "It has six bedrooms," she said. "Every one of them has its own TV, and four of them have their own bathroom too."

"I bet you get through a bit of bathroom cleaner!" I smiled as the lift door slid open.

Sonia laughed. "How many bedrooms have you got in your house?" she asked.

"One," I said.

"And how many people sleep there?"

"Four of us."

Sonia nodded as she unlocked the door into the apartment. It took three different keys.

Straight away, I felt as though I was in a film.

We crossed this massive living room with a carpet so thick and squashy it was like walking on the beach. On one side was a stereo, a home-cinema that took up about half the wall, and a fireplace made of glass with armchairs around it.

Further along there was a dining table so shiny you could see your face in it, and a sofa that looked as though it was made out of sugar.

"Who lives here?" I asked. "The richest woman in the world?"

"No," said Sonia, "but she's probably one of the richest women in São Paulo. She works for the television. She has her own programme ... on cable."

"Wow!" I said. "She must be as clever as anything!"

"Oh no," said Sonia, turning down her mouth, "she's as daft as a brush. But I don't tell her that!"

I walked through to the kitchen. It had everything in it: two fridges, a cooker about the size of a car, an automatic washing machine, and all sorts of gadgets and knick-knacks for making coffee, cocktails, pancakes and I don't know what else. I stood there, staring, as Sonia bustled past. All we had in our kitchen at home was an old cooker, a dented fridge and a sink to wash the dishes and the clothes in.

I walked through the kitchen and out onto a big balcony.

  While Sonia put the cloths into the
washing machine, I gazed down on the city.
Lines and lines of pale tower-blocks. The
sound of hundreds, thousands of cars stuck
on the roads. And, far below, Mr Oswaldo
still shuffling up and down at the traffic-
lights.

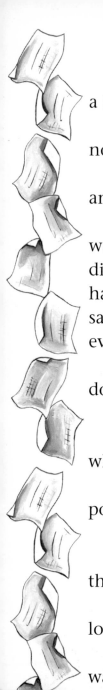

"You hungry?"

I looked round. Sonia was pulling open a big silver fridge door. I gave a shrug.

"Go on," she said. "No one will notice."

She heated up a plate of rice, beans and chicken, and I sat down at the table.

There was so much on the plate that I was still eating when she took the dishcloths out of the machine and started hanging them out to dry. I remember her saying, "On a hot day like this they won't even take half an hour."

And then we heard the key in the door.

"That's her!" said Sonia.

"What'll she do when she sees me?" I whispered.

"She'll go hysterical! She'll call the police! Hide!" said Sonia.

"What about this plate?"

"Just get out of sight!" hissed Sonia, as the second lock clicked.

"And the dishcloths?" I whispered, looking around for somewhere to hide.

I thought about jumping into the washing machine but I wasn't sure I'd fit.

I thought about climbing up the chimney but reckoned I'd probably fall straight down.

I spun round as I heard the third lock click open. I ran across the living room and dived under the sugary sofa.

The door closed and a pair of legs in smart trousers came swishing towards me. They stopped right by the sofa. I thought my feet must have been sticking out. But no.

"Sonia?" quavered a voice that sounded strangely familiar.

"Yes," said Sonia's voice. "Still finishing off Madam's cleaning."

"Oh, I'm awfully shaken up," said the woman. "I've had the most terrible experience. A boy at the traffic-lights stole my purse … "

So then I knew whose apartment I was in! And it got worse.

"Oh, you don't know how sad I am, Sonia," the voice went on. "I didn't mind losing the money in the purse. But there was a ring in it. It belonged to my great-grandmother."

I put my hand in my pocket. Yes. The ring was still there. Well, I was already picturing what was going to happen when I got caught. Sonia out of a job. And my mum's face when she came to visit me in prison.

I didn't want that ring to be in my pocket. It was bad enough getting caught hiding under the richest woman in São Paulo's sofa, but getting caught hiding under her sofa with her great-grandmother's ring in your pocket! Curtains!

So I did something a bit mad. My brain wasn't working right. I reached out my hand and put the ring on the coffee-table.

Thank goodness Mrs Birdsnest didn't see. She'd gone into the kitchen and I knew the next question that was coming.

"Sonia! Why on earth have you got all those dishcloths hanging on the washing line?"

"Well," said Sonia, "those are … those are holy dishcloths."

"Holy dishcloths?" said Mrs Birdsnest.

"Yes," said Sonia, and I started praying that she could invent a good story.

"You see," she went on, "in front of the house where I was born there was a statue of Saint Ozária of the Overflowing Fountain. One day the statue started crying. Tears came from the statue's eyes for three days and three nights. They formed puddles in front of our house and my mother had to use all these dishcloths to mop up the puddles."

Underneath the sofa I had to squeeze my nose to stop myself laughing out loud. Sonia hadn't finished yet, though.

"Well, today is Saint Ozária's day. Every year, on Saint Ozária's day, I take the dishcloths with me. And every year, miracles happen."

Mrs Birdsnest let out a little shriek.

"They're all wet!" she said.

"It's a miracle," said Sonia. "It happened about half an hour ago. They just went wet on their own."

"I see," said Mrs Birdsnest. "Well, excuse me, Sonia, but I'm really very tired. I'm going to have a nap."

That raised my hopes. I thought she'd go into one of the six bedrooms. But no. Her footsteps came across the room, and she flopped down on top of me on the sofa.

62

I knew what was going to happen next. There was a moment's silence. Then there was a really big scream.

"My ring! It's here! Oh!"

Sonia came into the room. "It must be another miracle," she said.

"Sonia!" said Mrs Birdsnest, wriggling around above me. "That ring was in my purse! I know it was! It really is a miracle! It's something for television! You must come on my TV show! I'll interview you about these dishcloths!"

"I don't know … " said Sonia.

"We pay!" shrieked Mrs Birdsnest. "We pay everyone we interview five hundred Reais! You must say yes! The viewers will be on the edge of their seats!"

"Well … " said Sonia.

"Say yes!" said Mrs Birdsnest. "I'll pay you now. Look."

Mrs Birdsnest got up and Sonia must have nodded or something because, next thing, a drawer was opening and Mrs Birdsnest was handing her the money.

"That's decided, then," she said. "Oh, I've come out all over in a sweat. I'm going to take a shower."

Off she went, and as soon as the bathroom door closed, Sonia was hustling me out of the flat.

"Looks like you've sold your dishcloths!" she said. "Go on. Take this." She was holding out lots of money.

"Don't be daft!" I said. "They're only worth twenty Reais!"

"Not now they do miracles!"

She handed me the money and, as the lift door was sliding shut, she looked into my eyes and laughed that lovely, mischievous laugh of hers.

It was two hundred and fifty Reais she gave me. As the lift went down, I started wondering whether to stop on the way home and tell Mr Oswaldo he could eat his hat.

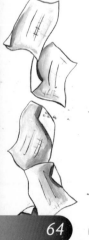